THIS
BOOK
BELONGS

TO_____

Disney's
SMALL WORLD LIBRARY
RICHES IN THE RAIN FOREST
An Adventure in Brazil

GROLIER ENTERPRISES INC.
DANBURY, CONNECTICUT

Developed by The Walt Disney Company in conjunction with Nancy Hall, Inc.
ISBN: 0-7172-8227-9

Huey, Dewey, and Louie were standing on a balcony before a magnificent view of Rio de Janeiro, Brazil's biggest city. Beyond the skyscrapers lay the beautiful harbor, dotted with boats.

"That must be Sugar Loaf!" said Dewey, pointing to the tall mountain that towered above the city.

Uncle Scrooge was in Brazil on business. Huey, Dewey, and Louie had come along for some fun. They were attending a party at the home of Mr. Saldano and, as usual, Uncle Scrooge was trying to make a few deals.

Scrooge stopped talking when a well-dressed gentleman swaggered in.

"Good evening, Mr. Saldano," said the gentleman. "I hope I am not too late."

"Why, of course not," replied the host. "It is always a pleasure to see you, Mr. Da Luz."

When Mr. Da Luz went to get some food, Uncle Scrooge turned to their host.

"That man must be very rich," said Uncle Scrooge. "I've never seen such expensive jewelry and clothes! Can you tell me how he made his fortune?"

"Black gold," said Mr. Saldano. "For many years, some Brazilian families made their fortunes from black gold found in the rain forest."

"Hmmm," Scrooge said to himself, "black gold is another name for oil. This trip may turn out to be more profitable than I thought!"

The next morning Huey, Dewey, and Louie were up bright and early. Uncle Scrooge had promised to take them sightseeing, and they were eager to see more of the beautiful city.

"There's been a change of plans," announced Uncle Scrooge. "I've hired a guide to take us down the Amazon River through the rain forest."

"Yippee!" cheered Dewey. "When are we going?"

"Our plane leaves in an hour," answered Uncle Scrooge.

"Let's leave right away!" cried Huey. "A jungle adventure sounds like fun!"

But fun was not what Uncle Scrooge had on his mind at the moment. He was thinking of one thing and one thing only—black gold!

Manuel, their guide, met them at the airport and took them to his boat at the river. Before long he was guiding the boat down a small tributary.

"Hold on!" said Manuel. "There's some white water coming up."

"Look at those rapids!" shouted Dewey. "This is going to be a wild ride!"

"Better than a roller coaster!" added Louie.

Manuel navigated the boat into the Amazon, moving around giant water lilies that covered the river like green blankets.

"Look over there!" said Huey. "A crocodile!"

"That's called a caiman," said Manuel, just as the animal opened its powerful jaws and snapped them shut on a dragonfly.

Suddenly something bumped the bottom of their boat.

"What was that?" asked Dewey in a worried voice.

"Probably a manatee," said Manuel. "They're also called sea cows."

"I don't see any cows," said Louie, who hadn't been paying attention to the conversation. He looked along the riverbank for a glimpse of the cows as everyone else chuckled.

Everyone but Uncle Scrooge, that is. He was also scanning the landscape—trying to imagine it covered with oil wells!

"Manuel," said Uncle Scrooge, "let's stop the boat now and look for oil—I mean, soil! Soil to stand on, that is." Scrooge didn't want anyone to know his plan just yet.

While the others set up camp, Scrooge went off to search for oil. He stuffed a shovel into a backpack and made sure no one followed him.

Scrooge stopped when he found what looked like shale, rocks that hold oil. As he began to dig up the earth, an army of ants came rushing out.

"Yeow!" screamed Scrooge, as he thrust his shovel into his backpack and ran back to the camp.

When he got there, Scrooge told Manuel about the little insects.

"Those were fire ants, Scrooge," said Manuel. "Their sting can be very painful. Even the anteaters stay away from them!"

But Scrooge kept his mind on business as usual.

"I'll just have to find another place to dig," he thought.

As he was about to go prospecting again, a thunderous sound roared from the jungle.

"Climb up!" shouted Manuel, shinnying up the nearest tree. Scrooge and the boys scurried up nearby trees.

"It's a stampede!" said Louie as a herd of wild pigs ran into camp. They all watched as the peccaries began to root around in the dirt.

"What are they looking for?" grumbled Scrooge.

"Food," said Manuel. "They can be quite ferocious, especially when they're hungry. We'll just have to wait here until they're done eating."

Scrooge sighed impatiently. He just had to find the black gold—before someone else beat him to it!

The next day Scrooge was so eager to begin exploring that he got up at the crack of dawn. He tried not to wake the others, but a butterfly landed on his nose and tickled him. "Ah-choo," sneezed Scrooge, waking Manuel and the boys.

"That's an eighty-nine butterfly," explained Manuel as the creature floated away. "Look at the pattern on its wings and you'll see why."

"Hmm," said Scrooge to himself, "this could be a sign of good luck. Maybe I'll make 89 million dollars from black gold!"

Manuel interrupted Scrooge's thought. "Are you ready to hike deeper into the forest?"

"Please, Uncle Scrooge!" begged Huey.

"All right, lads," answered Scrooge, secretly pleased that he would get another chance to search for the black gold.

As they were walking, Scrooge noticed a group of people through the trees. They seemed to be studying the ground.

"Aha!" thought Scrooge. "Maybe they're looking for oil, too."

Scrooge walked up to the group. "Hello, there," he said, "I'm Scrooge McDuck. You wouldn't be looking for anything *valuable* in this rain forest, would you?" he asked, winking.

"We sure are!" replied one of the men, who introduced himself as Dr. Lemos. "We're looking for things that will make people feel better."

Scrooge beamed, thinking about how wonderful money made him feel. "Would you mind if my group and I joined you," asked Scrooge, "and shared whatever discoveries we might make?"

"Not at all," said Dr. Lemos. "We can use all the help we can get. Tomorrow we're moving to our next campsite. It's five miles down the river. Let's meet there in the morning."

The next day, Scrooge, Manuel, and the boys headed down the river. When they got to the site, their new friends were already waiting for them.

"Don't wander off," Manuel warned Uncle Scrooge.

"That's good advice," agreed Dr. Lemos. "You should always stick with a companion when you're exploring a new place."

Dr. Lemos helped Manuel and the boys unload the boat and put up their tents. Once again, Scrooge slipped away unnoticed.

"I can take care of myself," Scrooge thought as he looked around for a place to start digging. "Besides, if I find the black gold by myself, then I won't have to share it."

Scrooge cleared away a small area and began to dig. He thought about how rich the oil was going to make him and began to whistle a happy tune.

A growling noise yanked Uncle Scrooge out of his daydream. He turned around slowly. There, just a short leap away, stood a large jaguar!

"H-h-h-help!" yelled Scrooge as the jaguar roared at him. But Scrooge's voice came out as a whisper. As he stood frozen in fear, Dr. Lemos rushed into the clearing

with several of his workers. They began making loud noises to try to scare the jaguar away. Luckily for everyone, their plan worked. Giving one last roar, the jaguar trotted off into the jungle. Two baby jaguars jumped out of the bushes and followed.

"Whew! That was a close one!" said Scrooge. "How can I ever thank you?"

"The jaguar was only protecting her cubs," said Dr. Lemos. "You're lucky we heard her roar. You shouldn't have strayed from the camp."

When Scrooge and the others got back to camp,
Manuel and the nephews ran up to meet them.

"We were worried when we couldn't find you,"
Manuel said to Scrooge.

"We looked all over for you," said Huey.

"I'm sorry," replied Scrooge. "I guess I got carried
away. I was trying to find the black gold and keep it all
for myself."

"Black gold?" asked Dr. Lemos. "That's not what we're after. We're scientists and we're looking for rare plants and flowers. You see, many medicines come from plants found only in the rain forest."

"You're looking for medicine?" Scrooge asked increduously. "Well, I guess medicine is more valuable than black gold," he admitted sheepishly.

"Much more valuable!" agreed the boys.

"But why were you looking for black gold in the ground?" asked Manuel, staring at the shovel that Uncle Scrooge had removed from his backpack.

"Because that's where you find oil," said Scrooge.

Manuel shook his head. "In this part of the world, black gold isn't found in the ground," he said. "It's found in rubber trees."

"In rubber trees?" asked Scrooge in disbelief.

"That's right," said Manuel. "In Brazil black gold is another name for rubber, not oil. At one time it was a very valuable crop, but now most rubber comes from Asia. There are no more rubber plantations in Brazil."

"I guess this has been nothing but a wild goose
chase," grumbled Scrooge.

"Don't you mean a wild *gold* chase?" asked Louie.

"That's it!" laughed Scrooge. "It's been a wild black-
gold chase. But it's certainly been an adventure I'll never
forget!"

Did You Know...?

There are many different customs and places that make each country special. Do you remember some of the things below from the story?

Rio de Janeiro is known as Brazil's "Marvelous City." Rio's beaches, wonderful museums and gardens, and famous Sugar Loaf Mountain make it one of the world's most beautiful cities.

Carnaval is Brazil's biggest and brightest holiday, and it lasts for a few days during late winter or early spring. In every city and town people dress in colorful costumes and parade and dance through the streets.

The Amazon River region is a wildlife paradise. It is home to thousands of different kinds of animals, birds, fish, and sea creatures unlike those found anywhere else in the world.

Next time you take a deep breath, think of the Amazon rain forest. Its plants and trees give off about half of the Earth's oxygen.

Brazil is the only Latin American country where Portuguese, not Spanish, is the official language.

"Adeus" (ah-dyuws) means "good-bye" in Portuguese. "Adios" (ah-dee-ohss) is how to say "good-bye" in Spanish.

Fire ants are very common in Brazil. They live in mounds that are two feet high. If a person or animal disturbs the mound, thousands of ants will attack, stinging the intruder with painful venom. Run, Scrooge!

The jaguar is the biggest and most powerful wild cat in North, Central, and South America. This spotted animal is able to see well in the dark, allowing it to roam at night as it hunts for other animals.

Rubber, which was once considered Brazil's "black gold," is now grown in Asia. Latex, from which rubber is made, comes from the rubber tree. Workers cut grooves in the tree bark so that its white juice runs out. This juice is collected in pails and combined with other chemicals to make rubber. Synthetic rubber is made in factories.

The Brazilian sport of *capoeira* (ca-pway-rah) is unlike any other sport in the world. It is a colorful blend of dancing and judo. Once a dangerous kind of fighting, capoeira is today considered an exciting form of folk dancing.

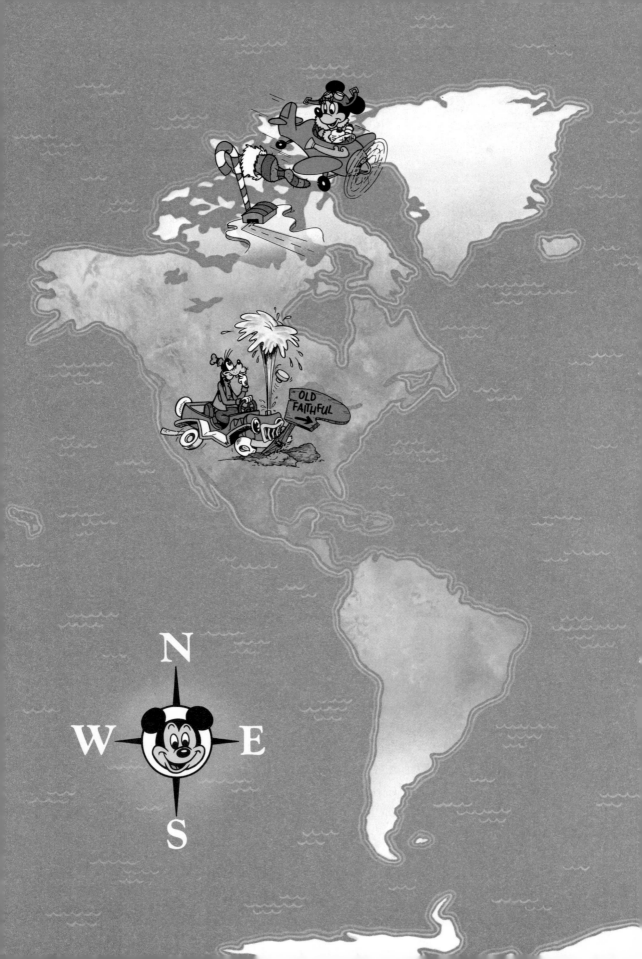